Cataloging-in-Publication Data (by Cassidy Cataloging)

Otoshi, Kathryn.
Baumgarten, Bret.

Beautiful hands / text by Kathryn Otoshi & Bret Baumgarten;
illustrations by Kathryn Otoshi. -- Novato, CA : Blue Dot Press, [2015]
   pages : illustrations ; cm.
   ISBN: 978-0-9907993-0-6
   Audience: Ages 3 and up.
Summary: Little hands can do so many wonderful things: *plant* ideas; *lift* spirits; *stretch* imaginations.
This colorful concept book rouses childrens to use their hands for the good and reach for their dreams. -- Publisher.

1. Hand--Juvenile literature. 2. Hand--Art--Juvenile literature. 3. Thumbprints--Art--Juvenile literature. 4. Handicraft--Juvenile literature. 5. Arts and children--Juvenile literature. 6. Creative ability-- Juvenile literature.
7. Creative thinking--Juvenile literature. 8. Inspiration--Juvenile literature. 9. Imagination--Juvenile literature.
10. Plays on words--Juvenile literature. 11. [Hand. 12. Hand--Art. 13. Thumbprints--Art. 14. Handicraft. 15. Arts and children. 16. Creative ability. 17. Creative thinking. 18. Inspiration. 19. Imagination. 20. Plays on words.] 21. Children's stories. I. Title.

PZ7.O8775 B43 2015
[Fic]--dc23   1509

BLUE DOT PRESS

17 San Pablo Court
Novato, CA 94949
www.kokidsbooks.com

Distributed by PUBLISHERS GROUP WEST
1-800-788-3123

Printed in China
by Prolong Press Ltd.

Beautiful Hands

Kathryn
Otoshi

Bret
Baumgarten

What will your

Will they

LANT...

What can you plant?

IDEAS?

Or TOUCH...

What can you touch?

HEARTS?

Will they  LIFT...

What can you lift?

Or STRETC

What can yo

stretch?

...utiful hands DO...

"My hope is that
this book empowers creativity,
compassion, love and connection
to you and yours, in the fulfilling and
remarkable way it has for me."

~Bret Baumgarten 2014

About the Story & Illustrations

This story is based on Bret Baumgarten's experience of holding his children's hands in wonder and asking them, *"What will your beautiful hands do today?"*

His question led me to reflect upon Bret's deep love for his family and friends, and his innate ability to touch and connect with others, both with his heart and physical touch.

Thus the realization of what little hands could do became two-fold: while our hands can do many wonderful physical things – *touch, stretch, reach* – when they are simultaneously used with good intentions, all these actions can add up to a much greater unforeseen vision.

The handprint illustrations in this story are made up of Bret's family and my own. The rainbow spread at the end of this book embeds the handprints of over a hundred family members and friends.

"Thanks to those of you who gave the gift of your beautiful hands
in loving support of our story behind the story." ~K.O.

AUMGARTEN

n our hearts ~

014

DEDICATED TO NOAH & SOFIE *"Reach high!"*